MY SPIRIT SOARS

Lots of Love and Respect
may the Great Spirit
Love and Protect you
to the End of time

Hatha Squalem, te na thaw

Chief Dan George
Tanyal, Staleston

My Spirit Soars

by Chief Dan George
and Helmut Hirnschall

HANCOCK HOUSE PUBLISHERS

ISBN 0-88839-154-4

Copyright © 1982 Chief Dan George & Helmut Hirnschall
1986   Fourth Printing

Cataloging in Publication Data

George, Dan, 1899-1981
   My spirit soars

   1. Hirnschall, Helmut. II. Title.
   PS8563.E59M93 1981   G811'.54
   C82-091113-5   PR9199.3.G45M93 1982

Cover Design Peter Burakoff
Printed in Canada by Friesen Printers

Published simultaneously in Canada and the United States by

HANCOCK HOUSE PUBLISHERS LTD.
19313 Zero Ave., Surrey, B.C. V3S 5J9
HANCOCK HOUSE PUBLISHERS INC.
1431 Harrison Avenue, Blaine, WA 98230

Contents

Friendship lives in every heart.

Never have the animals been in
greater need of human compassion.

Have I Left the Eagle to Soar in Freedom?

The time will soon be here when my grandchild will long for the cry of a loon, the flash of a salmon, the whisper of spruce needles, or the screech of an eagle. But he will not make friends with any of these creatures and when his heart aches with longing he will curse me.

Have I done all to keep the air fresh? Have I cared enough about the water? Have I left the eagle to soar in freedom?

Have I done everything I could to earn my grandchild's fondness?

There Is a Longing

There is a longing among all people and creatures to have a sense of purpose and worth. To satisfy that common longing in all of us we must respect each other.

In the olden times man and creature walked as friends who carried the beauty of the land in their hearts. Now each one of us is needed to make sure the salmon can find a place to spawn and the bear cub a tree to climb.

There is little time left and much effort needed!

Prayer for My Brother the Bear

O Great Spirit who listens to all
I speak for my brother the bear:

Make the moon shine softly during the nights of his childhood so that the warmth of his mother will always be in his memory.

Make the berries grow in abundance and sweetness so that the vigor of life will strengthen his heart and the years of old age shall never be a burden to his body.

Let the wildflowers refresh his temperament so that his manner will always be carefree.

Give his legs swiftness and strength so they will always carry him to freedom.

Sharpen the senses of his ears and nose so they will always keep harm from him.

Let only those men share his path who in their hearts know his beauty and respect his strength so that he will always be at home in the wilderness.

Make men praise life so that no one needs to feel the shame that lives in a heart that has wronged.

Then my wild brother, the bear, will always have a wilderness, as long as the sun travels the sky.

O Great Spirit, this I ask of you
for my brother the bear.

The Bear is Closest to Man

When I was born my grandfather took me from my mother and wrapped me into a black bear's soft fur blanket. It gave me warmth! It gave me security and comfort! How can I be anything but grateful to the bear? Of all the creatures he is closest to man. Yet it seems there is little place for him now.

The Empty Loon's Nest

I have seen the sun burn off the early morning mist as many times as there are leaves on a dogwood tree. Just as often the stars have stood vigil over my dreams, and the seasons, with their coming and going, brought enough work to keep me from lamenting their passing. Many strange things have happened during my lifetime. Often I could not understand the changes. I have been angered by some, shamed by others, and saddened by many. But nothing can give me a greater feeling of loss than the way nature disappears to make room for people's pleasure.

Beyond the reeds of the lake where my cabin stands is a loon pair's nest. Season after season I have greeted their new chicks since I was a boy. I no longer go there because the sun shines on an empty nest that the rain and wind turned into a pile of sticks. The evenings are without the laughter of loons and I wonder where they are raising their young now.

Have they built their nest away from motorboats, foul-smelling water, and people who make them dive just for fun? Is there a quiet lake left anywhere? Who will bring us the messages from the spirit world when the loons are gone?

My Face is the Land

Many seasons ago my arms were strong, my spine straight, my legs had swiftness, and my eyes were as good as a hawk's. People would look at my face, and all they saw in it was the face of a nameless Indian. Few people called me brother. It was my face that kept them from wanting to know me better, because it was the face of an Indian.

Yet, already then, my face was well known.

It was known to the squirrel that heard a twig break under my foot while I walked into the woods.

It was known to the porcupine that sat in the tree top and watched me pass underneath.

It was known to the raven who cawed to other creatures to tell them of my coming.

It was known to the fox who stole from my food cache and to the beaver who watched me set traps.

It was known to the bear whose den and my house were in the same forest.

It was known to the heron who taught me patience in the quest for food.

It was known to the warbler whose song filled my heart with joy.

It was known to the wind that brought me messages from other creatures and plants.

It was known to the rain that feeds the spring where I quenched my thirst day after day.

It was known to the lakes whose waters blended with the sky who speaks to all of freedom.

The trees also knew my face. I was told by my father that some day, when the skin of my face takes on the furrows of pine bark, my spirit will leave my body and seek a new home in a tree.

But like the wolf that soon will be gone from here, my face is the face of a vanishing kind.

You see, what is in the wilderness is in my face, and what is in my face is in the wilderness.

My face is the land!

If you misunderstand one you will neglect the other!

If you harm one you scar the other!

If you despise one you will disgrace the other!

If you shame one you will cause the other to weep!

If you look at one and cannot call its name you will never know the other!

But how can you not know my face?

How can you not know the land?

Is it not all around you?

Is it not part of all you do and live for?

Is it not within your heart, where the yearning for brotherhood takes its beginning?

Are we not all living in times of enlightenment when no one should have a nameless face any longer, not even an Indian?

Now that my hair has the color of moonlight and my voice sounds like gentle winds blowing on dry leaves my face is known everywhere because of the magic of films. People point at me and say with admiration: Chief Dan George. But how many of my brothers still have nameless faces because they are Indians, as I once did before you knew me as Chief Dan George?

I've Tried to Be an Indian

Let no one deny me the right to say that I've tried to be an Indian.

In the White Man's world I found it difficult, but I've tried.

I've tried to care for my people and showed my concern as Chief Dan George, not how others wished me to show it.

Can the deer climb the tree like a raccoon? There will always be someone who confuses the deer with the raccoon, but such a person has slow eyes and a quick tongue.

And if someone says I have not been Indian enough he will never know how much I've tried.

Pity

Pity the old man whose children cannot hear his sighs.
Pity the old woman whose only comfort is a fading memory.
Pity a people whose aged cannot smile into the setting sun.

A child's trust in a
grown-up shows in the
touch of his hand.

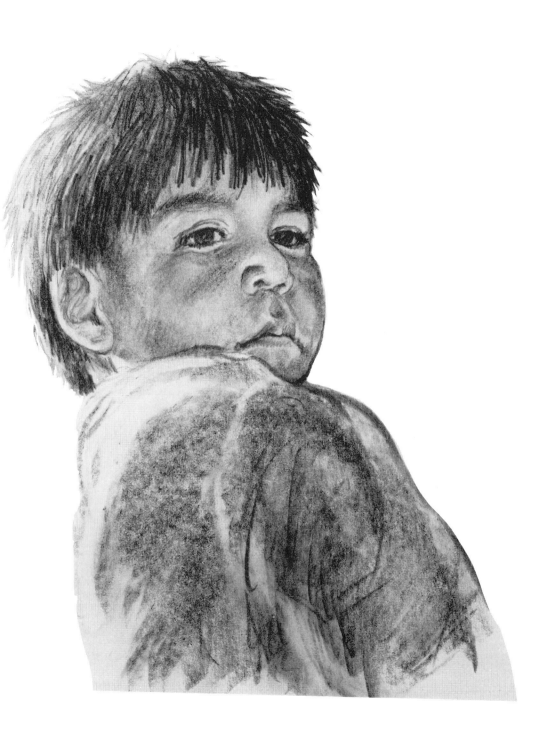

27

Let Nature Be

Is it really important for a boy to learn the name of a wild animal, what it eats, where it lives, and how it rears its young while at the same time the boy never gets to live near the animal? Would it not be better to let nature be, and let the boy live with unspoiled affection for all creatures, instead of teaching him to boast of knowledge?

The only thing the world really needs is for every child to grow up in happiness.

30

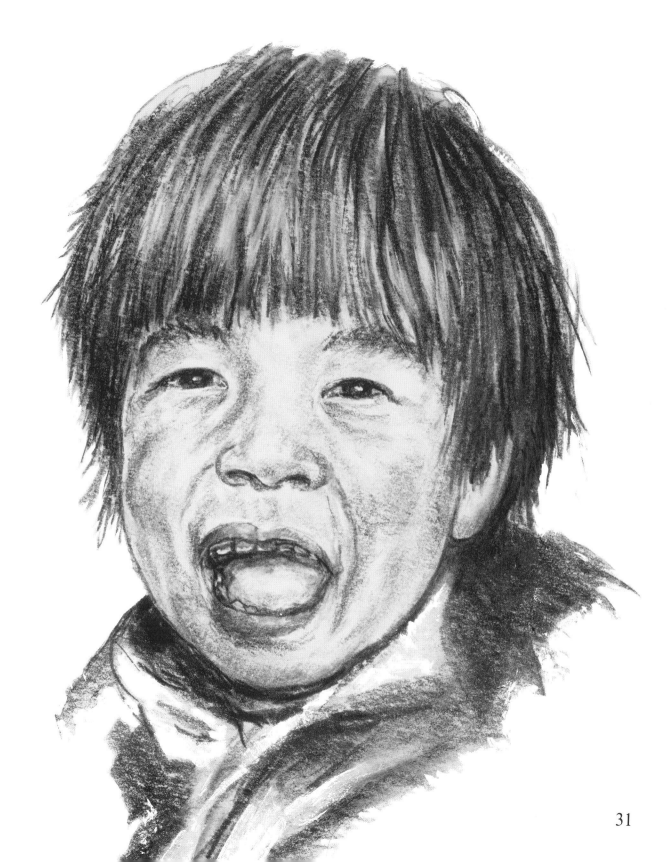

To a Native Teenager

You are unhappy because
you live far from the city
that promises everything and
you think yourself to be poor
because you live among your people.

But when you live like
a person of city breeding
you will not hear the plants say:
eat off me,
nor will you take
from the animals because of hunger.

The ground will be so hard
that you will want to run
from place to place, and
when you have gone too far
there will be no moss to rest on,
nor will your back find
a tree to lean against.

Your thirsty throat
will long to savor water
from the cup of your hand;
instead the liquid that lives in a bottle
will burn your tongue,
soften your mind,
and make your heart ache
for the sweetness of spring water.

Tears will keep your eyes moist
because a thousand small suns
that never come nor go
flicker everywhere.
The wind will not carry
messages from land to land,
and the odor of countless machines
will press on your chest
like the smell of a thousand angry skunks.

You will look at the sky
to pray for soft rain;
instead you will find
above the tree tops
lives another city
that stands between you

and the guidance of stars,
and you will wonder where city people
keep their dead.

A longing will rise in your heart
for the days of your boyhood, and
your fingers will grip the sacred tooth
you hid in your coat pocket.
But the train that carried you into
the city never brought the spirit along
that guides lost hunters through the woods.

Again and again your eyes will try to see
the evening dripping off the sun
like wild honey and your nostrils
will quiver for the scent of water
that tumbled through the canyons
of your childhood.

You'll stand at a corner
amidst the noise
and bow your head in despair
because you are humbled
by the desire to touch
your father's canoe
that he carved when you were born.

Wherever you look
there is nothing your eyes know,
and when weakness settles into your legs
you will recognize your brother
by the shadow his hunched body casts
in the corner of a street,
in a city where people walk
without seeing the tears
in each other's eyes.

37

© R80 Hirnschall

38

When Death Comes

Death will be gentle with me. Like an old friend dropping in to see me and asking me to come along for a stroll towards the sun. I will not hesitate to entrust myself into his company. I will not pause in my steps to look back.

Or perhaps it will come while I am sitting in my soft chair, wrapped in my blanket. I will not sigh, so that the others can go on with their business thinking me to be asleep.

I will know then what I always suspected, that death is not a mystery but a guide to birth. Birth—everything begins with it: child, plant, river, earth and sun, stars... that which we do not see or hear, the spirit life that some do fear.

The Earth Waits for Me

Nights bring me hindsight,
days bring me doing,
tomorrows bring me wishes,
yesterdays bring me wisdom,
  the moon vanity,
  the sky longing,
  the sun fear,
  and the earth?
  It waits for me.

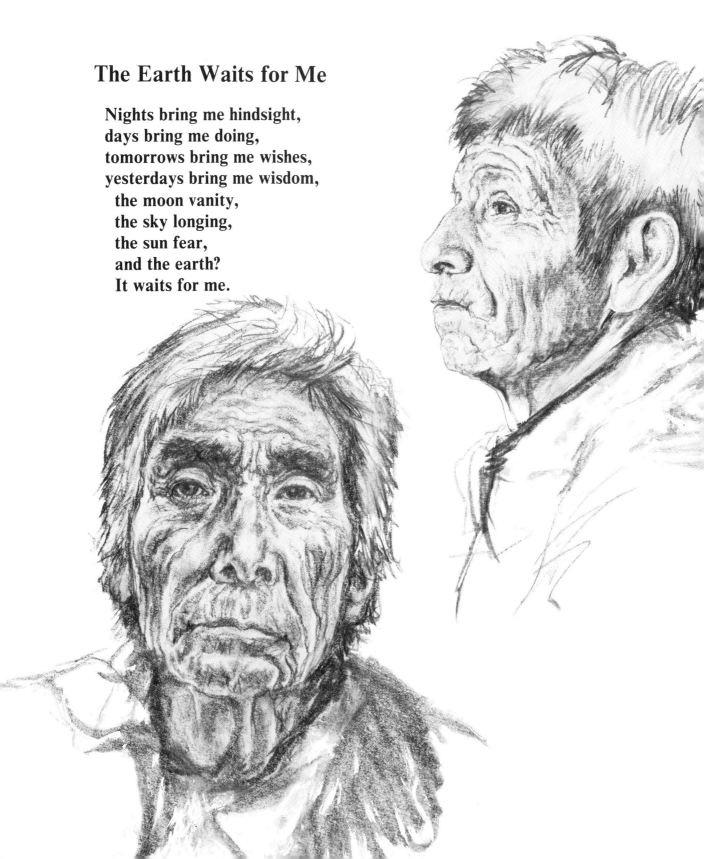

Death

Death comes to us in many ways.
It is in a broken flower,
in a carrot we eat,
or in a small child.

Death is ugly and beautiful.
It is useful and wasting.
It is tragic and happy.
It is in everything and
it is everything.

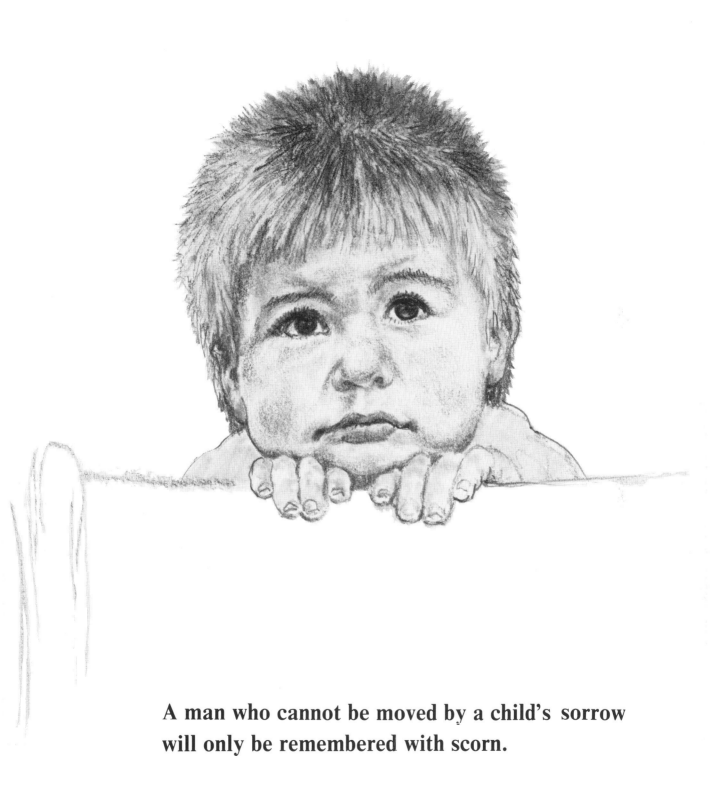

A man who cannot be moved by a child's sorrow will only be remembered with scorn.

It is a pity that an old man's
experience makes no
heirloom for a child.

My grandchild—you carry
my blood and shelter my
hopes.

The Wolf

The wolf has been driven from the land. Without him the wolf clan cannot celebrate the wolf ceremony. To lose a ceremony is to lose the past.

The Wolf Ceremony

I wanted to give something of my past to my grandson. So I took him into the woods, to a quiet spot. Seated at my feet he listened as I told him of the powers that were given to each creature. He moved not a muscle as I explained how the woods had always provided us with food, homes, comfort, and religion. He was awed when I related to him how the wolf became our guardian, and when I told him that I would sing the sacred wolf song over him, he was overjoyed.

In my song I appealed to the wolf to come and preside over us while I would perform the wolf ceremony so that the bondage between my grandson and the wolf would be lifelong.

I sang. In my voice was the hope that clings
      to every heartbeat.
I sang. In my words were the powers I inherited
      from my forefathers.
I sang. In my cupped hands lay a spruce seed—
      the link to creation.
I sang. In my eyes sparkled love.
I sang. And the song floated on the sun's rays from
      tree to tree.

When I had ended, it was as if the whole world listened with us to hear the wolf's reply. We waited a long time but none came.

Again I sang, humbly but as invitingly as I could, until my throat ached and my voice gave out.

All of a sudden I realized why no wolves had heard my sacred song. There were none left!

My heart filled with tears. I could no longer give my grandson faith in the past, our past.

At last I could whisper to him: "It is finished!"

"Can I go home now?" he asked, checking his watch to see if he would still be in time to catch his favorite program on TV.

I watched him disappear and wept in silence.

All *is* finished!

We are as much alive as
we keep the earth alive.

Life and death—a song without an ending.

Only love can stop a child from hurting.

We hurt the Great Spirit more than he hurts us!

If Your Soul Should Choose a Tree

The spirit world is connected to the world of breathing creatures. An old man can't be too happy about his afterlife. If his soul should choose a tree after it has left his body, what will become of it?

What future does a tree have nowadays?

The sun makes young people move fast and slows us old people down.

I Never Scorned God

My life has not been easy. There were
many ups and downs, good times and times I
lived with anger. All my anger was with people
about things that mattered only to people. I
never scorned God. My grandfather took great
care to teach me proper respect for God.

Our children must go to school to be
civilized. There they learn about churches. It
seems they have been built with the purpose of
finding fault with one another. When people
quarrel about churches they drag God into
their squabbles. My grandfather's church was
not built by men; therefore he could never have
taught me to quarrel with God. Our church
was nature.

A Bit of Sunshine

I enjoy sitting in the sun, although it no
longer warms me as much as it used to do
when I was younger.

I don't look about very much, and I
don't strain my ears to hear too much. There is
so much that I neither like to hear nor like to
see. So I just sit in the sunshine and enjoy
another quiet day.

Every time I lie down to sleep I do so
without knowing if another morning will come.
If it comes I say: "Good morning, world!" and
then I try to find a bit of sunshine.

Change

The world has changed so much that old people feel as strange in it as very small children do. Unlike a child who has no other choice I do not want to learn new sounds, new tastes, new smells, and new touches.

To others they mean progress; to me nature is still the best world to know. One cannot shake the olden days off easily.

61

We Have Lost So Much

We have lost so much. Although circumstances were against us, we are at fault as well. We did not know how to cope with the shock the white man inflicted upon us.

Honesty and Vanity

At my age a blanket and a comfortable chair to sit in are the things I need most. Time stretches and makes me mull over a lot of things. Some are not important; others will always carry weight, regardless of age. Like thoughts about honesty and vanity. Just like oil and vinegar, the two don't mix; yet I ponder the vicissitudes they caused. During my childhood, honesty was nurtured in every child. Now vanity has taken on the disguise of honesty and tricks many a parent into teaching the wrong attitudes.

I fear for my grandchildren.

I fear for the earth.

Man's vanity has the power to do away with all life and cause the earth to shake the foundations of the universe. Honesty, the kind that carries respect for life, is the only force to prevail over vanity.

My Soul

My soul—soon you will find
out how cold the sun is,
what makers weave dawn and
cause time to sing to man.

Where no one intrudes
many can live in harmony.

Hopes

Hopes?
Doesn't everybody have some?
There is one deep in my heart.
That something of myself remains behind as a bridge,
however small, so that some wanderer may cross over and,
while doing so, may sense the builder's deep feeling for
brotherhood.

No Longer

No longer can I tell my grandson: This is your land!

No longer can I say to him: Hunt, so you can feed your people!

No longer can I ask him: Pray in gratitude for there is abundance in the rivers and woods!

No longer can I cry: You are an Indian! Your future is good!

All I can do is hope.

May his years be peaceful and loving.

I wish every child can find its true path and every man knows the right way.

Wisdom

There is wisdom in youth and
there is wisdom in age.
One is loud and seeking,
the other is silent and true.

71

What Wonders and Hopes?

What wonders are children
expecting while we hand them
our problems?
What hopes do we nourish
in them while we are leading
them into despair?

The grace of God lives in a child's happy eyes.

All the scientists in the world will fail a child without love.

A child does not question the wrongs of
grown-ups, he suffers them!

Compassion

When you are old and left sitting by the side you may feel bitter. But bitterness drives warmth from the heart and makes you lonely. There was a time when I felt like that. Yet it didn't make me let go. Life still wants to be lived, and one does the best one can. The best way, the most gratifying is to look deep into the eyes of a small child. Look until you tingle with compassion. Then you'll see joy in life.

All the feelings one can have in the long years of life are to be conquered by compassion. Only then is one able to let the flame go out by itself.

Let Someone Else

I've made peace with the world and am grateful for
everything.
Let someone else greet the next spring with pleasure;
let someone else wrestle with another summer;
let someone else marvel over autumn's gifts;
let someone else say: "Life is good!"

Love

It is hard for a child not to be afraid.

It is impossible for a child not to be confused.

Our love can make a child look ahead with confidence.

84

To a Child

May the stars carry your sadness away,
may the flowers fill your heart with beauty,
may hope forever wipe away your tears,
and, above all, may silence make you strong.

The Right Kind of Love

The right kind of love, the silent, deep
and lasting one, pleases the creator.

Sometimes there may be darkness in our
hearts that makes us dread the future. Young
people should never overlook that this love is
working silently in a thousand ways. Because
of it we can have confidence in the years that
lie ahead. Wherever this love lives beauty
grows.

I would be a sad man if it were not for
the hope I see in my grandchild's eyes.

The Drum Has Fallen Silent

The drum has fallen silent,
the rattle lies broken,
the song has been forgotten—
my hands so feeble,
my voice so faint,
my eyes so full of tears—
O my grandson,
what will you remember me by?

Once More

Once more I like to hear water murmur of earth—
Once more I like to touch a child to feel beyond today—
Once more I like to taste a tree's sap to remember the
strength of spring—
Once more I like to see the color of happiness to know
the deathman's song will please me.
Then, O Earth, I shall be ready to return to you
what little I have left from all the years of taking from you.

Men who do not keep the earth sacred create much sorrow.

When my body lies without a song the eagle and my spirit soar together, and together they will cry for my people.

Grandchild, keep the eagle and the memory of me in your heart, so that both can remain aloft in peace, and together they will cry not of pain but of joy!

Epilogue
by
Helmut Hirnschall

The vicissitudes of life dealt Chief Dan George many a blow; the first was that he was born Indian. Like others of his race, he lived in poverty for most of his life. His Indian looks were his liability. When he reached his early sixties, this liability became his fortune; the Hollywood dream-makers discovered his face and turned it into a profitable asset. His quiet assertion, his whispering voice, his cascading white hair, his furrowed face with the gentle smile became a trademark for celluloid success.

Unlike many other people who are lured to fame and fortune by television or movies, Chief Dan George remained unspoiled. He retained his simple lifestyle and his faith in the principles that had guided him before. He continued to show respect for the Indian ways and nature, and above all he maintained his abiding love for his wife and family.

When the Chief received an Academy Award nomination for his performance in "Little Big Man," he and his wife planned to attend the ceremonies in Los Angeles together. Unfortunately, she became seriously ill. She insisted that he go to Los Angeles without her and watched the ceremonies on her television set from her sickbed. Her pride in him momentarily eased her pain. Death took her from him at a time when he ached to share his happiness with her.

In the following years, the Chief's star rose higher, and he acted before the camera next to such screen giants as Bob Hope, Glenn Ford, David Carradine, Clint Eastwood, Dennis Weaver, Art Carney, and Suzanne Sommers, to name just a few. He could not

fully enjoy his success, however, because his wife was no longer a part of it. Without her, he was no longer whole. His devotion to his wife, his longing to be with her, became stronger with every passing year. Near the end of his life he had withdrawn into the great emptiness her absence had created.

The last time I visited Chief Dan George I found him sitting in a chair in front of his house. A blanket kept him snug, the sun caressed him with warmth, the air bore the fragrance of summer. His eyes were closed, and so I approached him quietly. I dared not call his name or touch him lest I disturb his dreams. I wondered which lines in his face had been carved by hardships and which lines had been left behind by happiness. The skin followed closely the contours of his cheekbones, the mouth—emptied of its teeth—seemed without lips. The last few months had weaned so much from his body, everything about him said: It is time for me to let go.

I remembered a dream which I had had over a year ago. In it I saw him walk up the garden path to my house. At the front door we carried on a telepathic conversation. Shaking my hand, he declined to come inside and "told" me that he had come to say goodbye. I had been a good friend, and he thanked me for sharing his path. He would die in September.

During my waking hours I silenced my dream with doubts about its message. September came and went, and life stayed with him. I was glad my dream was no prophecy, and, like all other dreams before, this one too was quickly forgotten.

As I looked at him sitting in the chair while the sunlight played on his thin, white hair, a deep sadness took hold of me. Suddenly I knew my dream would be true; another September, only weeks away, would never end for him.

His eyes remained closed, but he seemed aware of me. Perhaps he had known all along that I was standing there watching him. He beckoned me to sit next to him, and I knew he wanted me to live out the words that he had dictated to me months earlier:

> Touch my hand
> before my voice will falter,
> sit with me
> until the shadows go,
> then smile....

Chief Dan George died the way he had always lived: quietly. His soul slipped from his sleeping body during the night of September 23, 1981.

As a small child he had watched his grandfather relocate their ancestors' bones and family relics. The new gravesite was farther up the Burrard Inlet, and the bones were transported in a canoe. As his grandfather paddled up the shore, seven porpoises appeared and followed alongside the canoe. Just before the canoe arrived at the shore where the new burial grounds were, the porpoises swam several times around the canoe and then dove and were never seen again. Dan George was told that the souls of his forefathers had been in those porpoises.

When Chief Dan George was buried, family and friends watched in awe as an eagle appeared overhead and flew, in silent circles. After the grave had swallowed the casket, the eagle disappeared into the clouds.

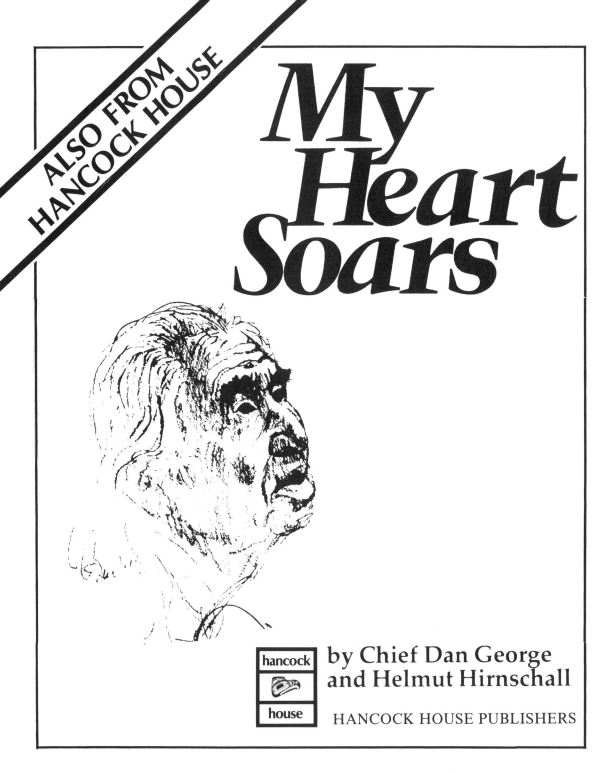

My Heart Soars

by Chief Dan George
and Helmut Hirnschall

HANCOCK HOUSE PUBLISHERS

A memorable collection of the thoughts and wisdom
of Chief Dan George,
sensitively illustrated by artist Helmut Hirnschall.